"Feathers on the breath
of a storm from heaven
whisked away in one direction only
and kisses snatched in passing
from one eternity into another."

~ Excerpt from
April and September
pg. 48

Also by Niels Hammer

The Art of Sanskrit Poetry (Munshiram Manoharlal Delhi)

The Importance of Hīnayāna and Mahāyāna.
Asian Philosophy

Affective States and Indian Aesthetics.
 Mind and Matter

Why Sārus Cranes Epitomize Karuṇarasa in the Rāmāyaṇa.
Journal of the Royal Asiatic Society

Eurasian Cranes, Demoiselle Cranes,
PIE *ger- and Onomatopoetics.
Journal of Indo-European Studies

Etymology of Sanskrit Kokiláḥ.
Zeitschrift der Deutschen Morgenländischen Gesellschaft

The Evolution of a Species-Specific term: Old Indic Krauñcaḥ.
Zeitschrift der Deutschen Morgenländischen Gesellschaf

Aesthetic Experience: Emotions and Reality.
Mind and Matter

STAGES

by

Niels Hammer

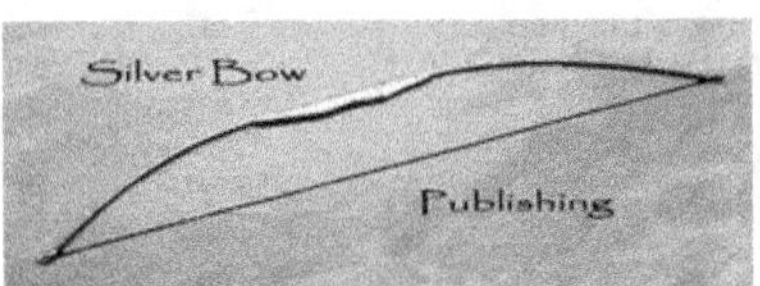

720 – Sixth Street, Unit # 5
New Westminster, BC
V3L 3C5   CANADA

Title: "STAGES"
Author: Niels Hammer
Cover Art: "People of the Foggy Surreal Cityscape" painting by Candice James
Layout and Design: Candice James
Editor: Candice James

www.silverbowpublishing.com
info@silverbowpublishing.com
© Silver Bow Publishing 2025
ISBN: 9781774033852 book
ISBN: 9781774033869 e book

Library and Archives Canada Cataloguing in Publication
Library and Archives Canada Cataloguing in Publication Title: Stages / by Niels Hammer. Names: Hammer, Niels, author. Identifiers: Canadiana (print) 20250269368 | Canadiana (ebook) 20250269392 | ISBN 9781774033852 (softcover) | ISBN 9781774033869 (Kindle) Subjects: LCGFT: Poetry. Classification: LCC PR9170.S83 H367 2025 | DDC 821/.92—dc23

To Yvonne

CONTENTS

The Tropical Forest

Night

Emerging above the evanescent surface
all at once aware, another metamorphosis,
past fusing present flowing slowly,
water wafting the skiff hither and tither,
the lifeline still clutching the broad-beamed
Neram Tree whose tangling roots
clasp the brink in compact embraces,
sustaining the soil, the tree itself
and the entire realm of insect,
fungus, moss, and avian species
in mutual coexistent evolution.

Aswim in a seething ocean of insect sounds
arising from nowhere and everywhere together
whitewashing the darkness, ebbing, and rising,
icicly pierced through by crystal calls —
a pompous Chanticleer claiming the night's
vast web and woof of leaves and new spidery nets
as his solemn castle estate, to sway the hens
who try his timbre on their perfect touchstone.

The water from the bottle tastes of fermented past,
flat droplets stick deadened to the close-knit net.
Plush puffs of sun-greened plants, worm-brittled wood,
soft rotten onion stench, and mangosteen perfume
spice each breath of air that fires the blood to flow —
revulsions and roses cross to form Janus-faced hybrids.

Above — a sky-broad stream, black infinite velvet,
besprinkled faintly phosphorescent,
acutely symphonic with spacious sunlings
shaping the xx lineaments on the face of love
between the canopies Dipterocarp's crowns.

There and there a vast constellation hides
a fleeting flicker behind the lateen-cut sail-wings
of sudden abrupt owl-moth maddened bats.

High-pitched monotonous croaking wails
from choirs of Horned Frogs rise refuted by shoals
of marauding Mahseers jumping for joy to transcend
the insubstantial gravity nothings of air.

A chill more glacial than chills of the night-dense dew,
edge-eery wails trail through lugubrious howls,
a Fishing Owl, a soul in torment eternal,
an unknown or even unknowable wraith,
a lost wretch attempting to leave or return,
marooned on the threshold darkness death throws on life.
Sounds and suggestions inebriate distinctions.

Shining on westerly waters the Moon's sail nigh striking,
the night-ripe atmosphere pregnant with her presence,
an aegis beneath which all that is living sprawls
within an invisible net of subtle-spun gravity,
with no hope of release before hauled homeward for good.

Throbbing rapidly drum-skin drrrrrrs,
the river-dense air played by ravenous Nightjars
engrossed in zig-zagging hunting lust
to catch woollen moths in their wide-open beaks
and quench the flapping whirrings of wings
by acid drowning and gizzard grinding.

Subjectively meaning is absolute,
universally absolute indifference.

Life may be naught but the second-best option
if trusting instinct or well-spun reason,
and chiselled in obsidian by action potentials -
a bitter-sweet comfort that day no choice is left.

Vocalic wauw-wauws — an Argus displaying his fan
of feathers to turn the mood ripe for the daylit dance
though darkness now closes as lids his all-seeing eyes
and the drowsy seraglio stays stoic till sunrise.

The high-pitched whining of vampires thirsting for blood
keeps ceaselessly sizzling outside of the net

and yet each single sucking sting
would contribute to sustain the symbiosis
the forest craves as a composite organism
evolving in harmony with the single source,
and constant itches craving constant itching,
and falciparum malaria, yellow fever —
so comfort, fear, convenience oust abstract altruism.

All ways out lead into the dead end
of the labyrinth if the way within is lost.

Air-creasing crickets grind sounds coarse-grained,
attention is hypnotised by monotony
till slurping splashes sketch a thickset mammal
thirst-slaking upstream at the eastern shore.

Metaphors, kennings, camouflaged correspondence,
may nudge some unstruck strands and strains to throb,
the near impossibility to tune the focus sharp
enough to invoke what this is in itself,
the urge to vie with Nature and create
regardless of how pale the ghost becomes,
the stubborn hope somehow to flesh the bones
and add a new aspect to the universe.

Each instant, the jungle night, too charged with sounds
to be internalised
except as fluttering fragments.
The present, which whisks emerging memories
away, is tuned too string-tense to shape associations.

Avalanche impressions of that which ex-ists
beyond the comprehending intellect —
reality — a Milky Way —
vast stretches appear or disappear
for instants or for ever.

To touch the light in the paintings of Vermeer,
to be the soul in the music of Bach,
to drip with the splash of a jumping frog in the dark.

The tightly interlaced coherence
entangling communion
when grace is granted by all six senses.

Dawn

And now this jungle night — it fades away
pale grey and weary of staying still as night,
fulfilled with its destiny,
and sun-drops drown themselves in blinding glare
behind the rising horizon.

A morning *rāgaḥ* dew-drenched, time and place unique,
though the theme has been played from aeon to aeon.

Large oval drops from drip tips of long-broad leaves
form in pools rings that ripple as rhymes
cresting the rhythm of the ground-swell scend.

The right-tuned self and splinters of insight
softly or strongly suffuse by volume and depth
neuronal connections as pulchritudinous thrills.

A Plaintive Cuckoo, exulting in awareness
of being alive right here this very Dawn,
far better than all past and future dawns
calls piercingly — glacial water clear vocals —
crowned by his cuckoo-kingdom of this earth,
alluring obsessively his faithless lovers
just to be faithful to him
for a cuckoo-quick all-encompassing instant.

This flow of events has never occurred before
now and will never appear again,
the pulse of premonition always sings this envoi.

A branch is roughly broken off a sapling,
an Elephant chews the juicy bark to shreds
insensitive to the sore survival leaves
as fertile pasture for blight and mould.

Drift-thinning mists — between Dipterocarps
that soar away from the wavy brinks of ferns

to brush their topmost leaves against the light —
are shades that sway away
above the watery way —
coy feline nymphs reluctant to sneak back to sleep,
nor ready yet to stretch themselves awake.

The water-heavy air creeps in through the cotton —
spirit and senses bask in the dawn of the jungle.

Gibbons, a family clan, sing daylight hymns
greeting each other to recognise themselves
before they swing their way through the tops of the trees
towards jujubes and rambutans to indulge
in the sumptuous feast the right brain hemisphere gives,
immune from the stoic stasis of surfeit;
each day more pristine than all yesterdays.

Now the twilight brightens even here
too quickly to catch the change of colours,
all tints and tempers metamorphose or deepen
to glow with an unearthly earthly sheen
as bliss in moments of pure buoyancy.

A Śambar belling, suddenly alert,
temple tin bronze cymbals loud and fey
a flute-clear warning
beware the threat of death
suspended in the awful still of silence,
and from beyond a diaphanous veil
of clarity a vision comes
of grace-black pupils, emerald-green eyes,
a lightning shadow darker than the shades
of night that still linger in the leave-dense undergrowth —
breathing stays postponed in indecision,
attention specifies instinctively
a fan of sedges behind the grassy ferns
appears to tremble without a touch of air,
the moment now without a sense of movement,
lengthening elastic till the silence snaps,
and wroth-hoarse raucous sawing bruise the air,
the stealthy stalking failed,

attempts now to remain
invisible of no avail
when focused sharply by all eyes and ears.

The freedom of consenting attuned to nature
grants fearless joy to hunt again at dusk.
Life plays with death and beatifies the tryst.

Snow-white slow-winged Egrets skim the water
surface as light seeps down through the depths to reveal
the movements of water-weeds that betray the fish.

From far away a lonely Jackal howls
this morning and existence in.
The depthless knelling of the sound,
the ticklish gooseflesh of a common mood
emerging from the periaqueductal gray.

Chaos puzzles time and space shaped events
into the only way they could
cohere in mutual interanimation —
interdependent evolution or
pratītyasamutpādaḥ.

Day

Anfractuosity of greenery,
three-dimensional mosaic of night -
dark secrets and sun-green leaf epiphanies
can close the gaping lips of wounds from loves
unanswered like calls caught in bottles dropped at Sea.

The undulating flights of Black-naped Orioles
weave invisible threads beneath the canopy
to echo the knitted hammocks of their nests,
the wavy flute-trill whistles of their calls —
long cool and liquid draughts of clear blue light,
extolling how again to-day they feel
intuitively grateful and content to be,
to see, to fly, build nests and mate and die.

Caw-winged dragonflies, yellow-black danger,
scratch the clear air near the ear opaque
with synchronised vibrating wing beats,
to rob the busy dipteran highways of life.

Where they went down to drink the pale blue smell
of Śambars hesitate to leave the leaf-cooled air.

Ripe fruits plop drown in the river as showers of hail —
the morning spill from banquets of fast-raiding birds.

The steely ways of dead-determined ants
criss-cross the smooth bark of Tualang Trees,
whose crowns are bristling with hives of nettled bees,
whose buttressed roots are twisting anchor dikes.
The two primaeval species of the forest
sustain the keynotes of the consonance.

Paddling leisurely upstream
without an inkling of doing
anything else or to reason why
the touchwood's scent of truffles
washes doubts and questions
away in a bath of euosmia.

Violent ripples ruffle the river's serenely
reflecting mirror along the western brink.
A pair of Smooth Otters take turn to nib at the neck
of a Python who lashing out from side to side
almost simultaneously tries to snare
them both to tighten her muscular coils
around their furious struggles to escape,
for later at ease to bask in the sun
and digest the prey who would have met the fate
the harmony of the universe had found
right as revenge for bold displays of hybris.

The exulting challenge thrill all through
each of their acrobatic twists and turns
to dodge the trap of her back-hooked teeth.
The gnawing nibbles will soon interrupt
neuronal transmissions and leave her paralysed
unless they should tire of the game or come
across a shoal of Carps.
As life plays thus with death
Atropos could just cut this thread as that.
The tragic comedy of life
is staged by a throw of dice.

Deep wedge-shaped sculptures in the soft dark clay
show the staid habits of a Tapir's life
until the next monsoon. The bygone night
that was alive and dark has changed to light —
leaving a sketch in snow and charcoal.

Round flexible leaves float islets on the surface,
a two hundred-million-year-old evolution
perfecting adaptation where air and water meet,
magnanimous sun shields for water snails,
and lees for silvery Barbs alert with hunger.
Life thrives at thresholds,
in far-from-equilibrium conditions,
beneath the shields of shadows
or on a float of mortice and tenon joined timber.

Each individual propagates the species
instinctively aware of former generations,
intent on fostering life of future offspring,
as single-minded as gravity or light,
anaesthetised to the grief of evanescence.

But there — from a knotty branch with silk-light leaves
closed milk-white flower udders
strut upwards together with green prickly pears —
and then the gooseberry garlic ripe
and strawberry rum-sweet fragrant
fruit opens to waft across time from the past
a wave that overwhelms the breath
with flavour fertilisation.

Each individual, not the species,
is expendable in the ceaseless process
Nature of reincarnation, metamorphosis,
new life, new events, new experience,
movements, to move and be moved.
Mountains which rise up by tectonic pressure
are ground to sand and dust by rain and wind.
Comprehension may form a semblance of meaning
in fragments in convex or concave mirrors.
Insight joins all points of the periphery
when the paddle is lifted
almost the same equilibrium returns.

A spotted Serpent Eagle, immobile as the Thingan
she hides in, waits for a Flower-pecker
to fly within reach, the best potential
to manifest itself before reaction.
Survival has strangely hidden causes
unless a sudden flash should illuminate
the way that lies stretched out ahead.
The day is too sky-blue to cloud potential fear.

Screaming, a Peafowl, fluttering wing beats
right through close foliage, fear-fraught warnings
a Muntjac barks — sudden silence broods
pregnant and ominous before the thunder bursts —

the still air quivers with the rising roar
of *aoum*, the infrasound deep water pressure
against the skin, the naked wistful yearning —
tangible empathy blesses living beings,
the soul that is shared, the difference is deceptive.
The full-throated purring ripples out through space,
a drawn-out vocalic and nasal euphony,
an echo of a conscious excitation
reflecting the wonder of an absolute —
a sky-blue mirror cloud-bedewed by breath.

Nothing, in itself, is inconceivable,
beyond the awareness of living beings
confined by the horizon of past experience.

Explosive puffs of dawn and midday flare
in corymbose sepals throughout the dusky green
as beacons for Grass Yellows, honeybees, black
and chalk white ants, all keen as death to drink
the nectar of life the birth tree of Buddha bestows
for the apotheosis of pollination.

One hundred and eighty degrees space colours
change into river purling euphonies
evoking ethereal floral-green fragrance
the senses cease to differentiate —
deluges of impressions dissolve
limits, definitions, and distinctions —
a right hemisphere neuronal symphony.

Slight listless eddies lick the sandy clay
where oval-toed broad pugmarks
beneath thick thrusting clusters
of satin-petalled orange-yellow orchids
with lazy lanceolate leaves
that cover the space-keen branch they have annexed
show that here a Tigress delights to still her thirst.

Seven essential affective dispositions
that motivate staying alive from breath to breath
engender the natural habit patterns

identical in Orioles, Tigers, sailors, and Gibbons.

Four boulder cloud shadows tiptoe softly,
mail-leather shielded from blood-hungry leeches,
behind the conjectures and green-bright leaf-screens
on crisply strewn moss towards the river's
harvest of raindrops, her cool-clear water blessing,
feeling at home, the Forest's birthright gift,
the pilgrim may strive with each pull of the paddle to share.

A stray Hibiscus flaunt blood oxygen-bright flowers —
densely humming wings, mild honey, dewy leaves,
a wraith from a bygone paradise unfurls
his spiral proboscis
delving violently down in through the nectar,
enraptured, fluttering space-black forewings
each flashing seven triangular dragon jewel
scintillating emerald teeth,
the hindwings flare rainbow-green broad brilliant bands —
a revelation of earthly ethereal beauty —
the feeling awareness subtle agony —
the seeing intensity a skyward fall
out into that which is becoming the seen
seen as it is itself.

The listener ceases to exist
transformed into sounds by the air
when the music no longer is heard.

A kindred close in to see, to know,
they touch antennae probing, smelling, sensing
to reach reciprocal recognition,
instinctively self-reflecting
to feel an irresistible urge
to whirl around each other exuberant to be
a dance of pure rejoicing in four fused dimensions,
flitting to and fro through foliage profusions,
diving or rising, flapping, or gliding,
to settle intricately spliced together
as an entangled pair
upon a curly fern,

reflected alive in the river pool's halcyon glance.

Dulled green triangles alight her greyish forewings,
sapphires spray the underside sky blue,
her wings are humming in creative
ecstasy of impregnation
and blue bliss lifts her up
to fly together with him towards eternity.

Thus, vindicating Teiresias.
To-morrow
she will, self-satisfied, fulfil her destiny
by laying one egg on each new-sprung birthwort leaf.

Mosquitoes can vanish in the air
if feeling exposed in the focus of attention.

Rhinocerotes adjust their birth rate
to stay attuned to the growth of grasses.

The oceanic nature —
a drop of individuality
awhile apart in symbiosis.

Each single event, each pristine impression —
a stone-shaped eddy,
an unrecognisable sound,
a startling glimpse, night-fathomless eyes
half-hidden behind a moving leaf —
marks that Pan watches, out of sight.
Sense, hearing, sight, and smell
are etched
indelibly into awareness,
leaving neither space nor time
for thoughts, associations, rest, or dreams.

The rainforests flourish
supreme diversities,
the infinite potential
of the form full Void.

So, seeing —
seeing the azure, blue brilliance
flushed with snowy feathers,
and seeing —
seeing the all-leafy greenery
exist in absolute aseity,
and feeling as keenly as possible
that the keening can continue deepening for ever,
and drinking in — absorbing reality,
with all the six senses perfect pitched
in as huge and eager draughts as possible
enough will never be enough
for universal thirst — immortal longings.

The pattern is thematic,
each evolution new,
the unique diapason
of this particular day.

A dwindling oasis in the wastes
of the spreading deserts of extinction.

Thus sings the south wind in the crumpling leaves.
Thus shape the clouds their funeral procession.
Thus points the drifting of the faintest stars.
Thus weeps the barren sea at the slag-strewn shore.

Thus fares the world engrossed in self-destruction,
in making a conflagration of its forests,
in leaving the surface of the Earth as ashes —
these ashes are all the inheritance the present
offers to vouchsafe the day tomorrow.

The way of the self,
true Nature trusts to hide.
Behind that which is present,
seen, thought, sensed, and heard,
the unreflected colours,
the unstruck notes,
the oceanic scend,
play hide and seek.

The Sea

Sepals of twilight fade away in grey,
Dawn glows rose petals orange to yellow,
a freshening west wind whistles thin-shrill tunes
in tightened strings of stainless shrouds,
the sounding wood vibrates anticipation
and moorings moan to brisk and choppy seas.

Waves break drumming the heartbeat of the Sea
upon the stretched-out shore to strum the joy,
hooves thunder across the shingle-buttressed sand.
bright manes of blue-black waves
torn off in tufts by boisterous gusts.
the note suffusing the air — wet seaweed salt.

A pristine day like no other past or future,
thus, and thus only as it is,
a presence arising out of absence,
a pitiless twang in the early born light to fare forth
out over the restless watery depths
toward something unknown in the looming horizon,
a light-shrouded breath, a shimmering haze,
calling as silence with twinkling twilight eyes,
to come, come hither, passing thoughts, to dare
dreading change, to seek out the spring of the rainbow —
the Ocean rush through the blood and the day-flushed Sky.

Unfurling the genoa flapping away to fly
away on sky wide wings of strained fury,
hoisting the heavy main sail haul by haul
and gleaning the peak eye ascending in the Sun's
through grids of shimmering eyelashes,
infused with the unknown, the rising onshore wind,
to sail the whale's way alone with the day,
this breathless instant of being light as light,
a breathless instant likewise as the darkness
that now as always waits prepared to pass,
as close to the wind as sails and keel can cut,
encountering each close embrace, each different wave
with open arms — a flurry of foam green seas
crashing in over the lacquer-gleaming gunwale,
sucked gurgling out through the self-bailing valves.

The feeling of sinewy shoals smooth-slipping seas,
the sense of the salt of the ancient Sea, more keen
than salt itself and fragrant dimethyl sulfide,
the whiffs of freshly growing brown-green seaweed
keep whetting my brine-wetted teeth.

Yet any search for any *Saint Graal* would be
a *Saint Graal,* in itself and self-defeating —
the edge gnawing rope of the sheet in the gusts,
the winch a relief, the cleat, the straightened leech,
just this, the Sea, the instant felt as it is.

Shedding the ring mail of proving some purpose,
kicking off the custom-forged habit of intentions
that shields against the feeling of the weather —
the main leech aspen shivers indecision,
falling off slightly to catch the air more cleanly
in tune with surging waves and williwaws,
defying heavy seas and dance inviting flaws,
daring them both to trust themselves more deeply
to thrill with exhilaration of the challenge,
to balance on tiptoe upon each razor's edge
though wary of such trysts in a cockpit of hybris.

Impetuous forces rush through the marrow of bones,
the stiffening gale, the whitening crests, the pull,
a birthright affinity with the primal timbre,
blinking too salty tears out of the eyes,
dodging the height and scend of steepening waves
to yield an inch or two to leeward
or clash through a splintering avalanche of crystals,
bear hugs of water, cat o' nine tails froth.

Each turn each twist, the rudder feels alive,
the thrust of the undertow, the play of fingers,
each tightening or slackening of sheets
a prerequisite for choices instants later,
pure predisposition or a warning impulse,
heeding the owl-soft wing beats of dread Angels.

The size, thrust and shape of a wave stay all its own

unless purloining power

from previous or posterior kith and kin
by quantum non-linear stealth.

A chill to the touch, a blink of an eyelid,
the balance of indeterminacity.
Imagining some present potential threat
might inadvertently chance to cause
a plume moth's hindwings to flutter
a puff of air that might change to a tempest.

The humour and tenor of a pirrie
newborn from the Sky to descend into the Sea —
a twofold inspiration for moves that thrive on air.

The frame of mind that's given and taken for granted
lays inadvertently two iron rails
all future thoughts and deeds cannot but follow,
the broad way of least resistance,
the nature of action potentials.
The innate limitations
of mindset, trends, and traits
christen the deadening weariness
that playing with wind and waves dispel,
creating a pristine brain plasticity.

This vast expanse of all-encompassing waters,
lullaby-cradling or shark-toothed with fear,
the fetch to the horizon that stays beyond reach,
steepening smiles of foam-crests from onrushing rollers
and green-black diamond lighted transparence,
sea scales splinter glittering prisms of mirrors —
hints to divine the features of a face,
to sound a rising mood
to choose the right options, amends of no avail.
The stage all set to windward, the day to turn dark,
timbre tones through the rigging thrilling with tension —
blind trust in its strength to sustain the strain
as trust in the fair view of a day tomorrow.

Large waves lift the hull up sideways
to surge in under the keel and pass to leeward,
the slide down smooth backs of charging Killer Whales
safe though still astounding gooseflesh shivers.
Now well clear of the coast, the twice wrecking limits,
tacking close hauled out towards a shoreless sea.
Stray whispers of fanned out cirri paint the blue fear pale,
forewarnings of a frowning of grim brows above.

Gusts flatten the sails — the backstay for balance,
clutching the thrashing tiller
battered by twists and turns of wilful waves
while reefing the jib to a liberal trysail.
A violent pirrie, a ninth wave could,
a mutual strengthening, a feed-back loop,
unconscious inclination, spores from the past,
glum clouds' mycelium, quickly rain-swollen
mushrooms within a fertile atmosphere.

The tilt all a trial, a challenge to thole
the ceaseless caresses sea-sailing grants.
Attention not flagging an eye lidded instant,
now seven and eight in the peak of the flaws.
A change in the tune of the morning's prognosis.
Dense banks of storm-driven clouds
sweep the soft smile off the lips of the Sky.
The day turns sullen already
as if with its back to the light from above.

The Sea pitch black, the foam hail icicles,
both cheeks stung livid, the fingers feeling numb,
the weather chills through the beat of the blood.
The light left gains an eerie sheen to windward,
the clouds congeal to layers
of bubble swelling purple breasts —
fell udders distended with beestings of torrents;
from saturated vapour grape-sized drops
condense — a waterfall — gasping for breath,
the waves crouch whipped flat beneath cascades of fury,
all frolicking air washed out of the foam,
incessant lightnings flash throughout the clouds,

a ghastly glow illuminates the waters,
but this is as it is, irreducibly real,
the feeling of staying one-sinewed with the Sea,
the black-light lap, the timeless now,
forever, and maybe tomorrow as well.

Exploding thunderclaps deafen ears to close,
pulsing air waves pressure, blasts of infrasound.
The danger of tempting lightning with a mast,
shattering timbers, loss of awareness.
Nothing but luck, hale fate or blind chance
or oak wood, varnish, and conductivity
of steel and aluminium and height of the clouds —
negative crystals of ice in lower layers
in upper layers positive graupel of hail
create the tension — ignition of lightning.

Lessening the risk leaves no viable options,
life vest and clinging to the wreck with shreds of hope
at best, or after a devastating struggle
the bitter acceptance of the sweetest of farewells.

Alone and abandoned to the Sea the true
nature of life or courage
may knell in harmony with the wind and waves.

Rearing, splashing, leaping chasms or drowning,
adjusting to stay upright, mute aching muscles,
this absolute, the desire to prevail,
the shared characteristic of all living beings,
appears as primaeval as nuclear forces.

Sustaining sky light still wards off the dark,
loosening, while it lasts, the lee jib sheet
and hauling the windward close to keep
the corner leech stretched out beside the shroud.
The rudder sixty-five degrees to windward,
lashing the tiller to the starboard cleat,
the mainsail stays almost aligned with the wind
and reefing blunts the slushing of the seas.

The speed slows, two knots, the drift uncertain,
stretching the fingertips up to touch the Sky,
the toes down to trip along the ribbed sea-sand
the strain subsides to seep out in the storm.

As wind and waves compose
harmonic rhythms for sail and rudder
life-born delight assuaging thirst and hunger,
pure water the best, a fire throughout the night,
earth-rich whole wheat golden crusted bread
and honey-bitter chocolate, alike lop-sided love,
in cockpit lee from foam and rain and wind
which still find ways to sneak
in under the oil cloth tightened armour,
and then the given offer to stay aloft and share
ripe sacred wine — upon wide purple wings
transcending gravity.

Flowing along the natural way as flotsam
and jetsam, stretched out on the leeward bench,
ubiquitous peace as presence
behind closed eyelids, heaving to,
dissolves the multiple focused points of space,
the sluggish stream of words and images
and slows down the heartbeat of time to fall asleep
as slowly the wrath of storms and seas abate.

The soothing cradle of long slow ocean waves
lulls gently the furious maelstroms of a nightmare
to a halcyon bliss from the womb of paradise.

An abrupt fall from the sky, the bench hits hard,
wrecked joints, strange chills,
some point of light did wink at the end of the tunnel.

A gibbous Moon changes prisms of shifting seas,
that catch the light, to silver mirrors scales,
the black remains transparent night-deep revelations —
the eyes of the water of the Sea,
the primal source of life,
the final gift of a fishy grave.

And thinking covers the rainbow hues of life
with apathy dark as loss or white as snow.

The brilliant beacons of the Seven Sisters
grant a wayward sailor a glimpse to follow fate
at ease while pitching along beneath their aegis.

South-easterly Betelgeuse flames red and fiery
against the frost of Rigel, blue-white, twenty suns,
Ōriōn, whom Artemis slew, his hunter hybris;
tales about Nemesis pale as lunar ghosts.

Behind the white imperceptible susurrus
of staying afloat or alive
a new-born silence might sense
how each star would sound in the symphony
of the Milky Way.

The wind lifts the jib, the bow turns to leeward,
the main sail tightens, the sea speed quickens,
the rudder nudges the prow up in the wind,
the main sail slackens; the jib feels all the air —
a cyclic water-wind dynamic process
shows that all is well with the present here in Heaven.

This Milky Way, three hundred billion drops,
illuminates the black potential of darkness,
the faintest discernible stars, sixth magnitude,
draw Deneb's two hundred thousand suns
down towards the Earth and mothers the immense
expanse of space that measures life and death,
that bitter-sweets the events of this blue-green sphere
all living being shares,
that gives the joy of sailing seas some salt,
that tunes each breath to echo waves and winds,
that fills an instant with universal depth.

But time is too Protean, a slippery shapeless,
to fasten in the coarse net of conception,
more fundamental, entanglement of two
paired particles, either space or time, not both.

Dawn's shortening colours charm the Night to sleep,
visions of conceiving a pristine day appears.

Closing the portals of gloom
sky-feeling fingertips
rose petals dewy;
maternally smiling
wavelets caress
the clinker-built sloop,
plum tongues, silk water
a latent potential,
the moon-piped tide,
this yellowing tint,
the Tea-rose thighs of Dawn
fragrance as light.

Waves ripple past, sails fill and flap,
a mother-of-pearl naked glowing shimmer,
where air moves water,
process and change
too multitudinous,
beyond still life attempts.

Trembling above the skyline
the Sun squints through eyelashes,
seeing, seeing the Sea as she stretches
herself out, three hundred and sixty degrees
to curve down towards the surrounding horizons
suggests the salient existence,
the bread and butter, the olive oil, the wine.
juxtapositions or hidden correspondence
may form individual or species-specific
perspectives - despair or exultation.

The waves spend the strength the wind inspired
on their way towards release on the coast —
the fish filter air out of water to breathe.

Loosening the tiller to turn round,
unfurling the jib to port,
hoisting the main sail up

to the top of the mast
and swinging the boom out to starboard —
the early morning wind
will breathe the sea-home shoreward.

This blood-red violent spheric realm of fire,
six thousand to twenty million degrees,
rising with the speed of the Earth spinning round,
fills the Sea with photons of life,
and fuses every single second
six million tons of hydrogen to helium —
the mother of death, before she dies so huge,
so hot, that the Oceans will boil away.

Each life, each phenomenon, lasts its allotted time,
and praise the coming as well as the going.

But not just now,
this day of days,
so strike the sails and throw off the clothes
and plunge down into the storm-purged waters
to absolute accept, a yielding close embrace,
a new well-known return to former life,
another mode of being slippery,
and not yet crystallised as denotations —
naked freedom, being all and nothing
yet spinning a lifeline, apotropaic magic,
aware of the shifting wind, the undercurrent,
the camouflaged fatigue, the spent potential,
this relaxation after strained attention.

Blue-yellow eyelashes drip-drop stings salt water,
buoyant and floating seaweed and kelp,
water feel caresses felt body boundaries —
the distinctions from the present vast and wet dimension,
the mammalian limitations,
sensing the primordial Ocean of life
as dread and awe, as care and flowing wonder,
dissolve when basking naked born
in the halcyon being of water —
before becoming too indifferent to care

shivering to dry in a bath of sunlight
reconstitutes the future,
grateful to that which is,
for having been granted a fleeting life to love
as well as a time to die.

April and September

The breath of soothing south winds thaws the snow
to trickles that return the sunshine,
winter-pale grasses feel naked and wet
beginning to green in light and air.
Fragrant vanilla night grained ice-cream
and ripe green apples with rosy heather honey.
Apotheosis by nature, evolution,
mushrooms feeling their way through earthy crust.
The soul of gossamer sinewy joys
throbs in the spinning.

Too souled to sense the pull of the Earth
flight-dance acrobatics twist and turn
flashes of night-day-bronze-green feathers
over the blue-sky ripple flooded meadows.
Silky leaflets of Willows, Sallows, Rowans
bath in the dewy haze at daybreak,
bursting with the coming in of Summer.
The full aseity of that which is
stuns imagination thunderstruck and wordless,
seeing, seeing it as the light it is,
each split of a second new — that which ex-ists
each now and here a universal centre
that which in its own time must pass away in peace.
Dancing round the spinning hub of gravity
four Seasons, holding hands, four warm, four cold,
celebrate the astral spring of fusion.

The early air is heavy honey, Dandelions
bloom in the sunlight as earthly echoes.
The Cuckoo stirs the soul from winter sloth,
vocalic, liquid, loud and clear, glu-coo,
the wistful blue bell of the springtime wood
tolling in exuberant choirs of warblers,
a spring melody spondaic in its blessing
one eighth of the oval path of the year —
the reverberations memories evoke,
stray tawny shadows of primaeval events,
a few with adamantine glimpses

aglitter still among the jetsam and flotsam
the tide of awareness washes to and fro.

A day burst forth — a green — green leaf unfurling,
a woman — susceptible rainbows
of gushing tears and pearly laughter.

Each laugh, each tear, painted another out —
the infinite canvas of time —
when lost in life and flapping in the lap of love.

II

The balm of intricately woven thoughts
ground salt-sea stings into the gaping wound
which childhood's loss of inner silence left.
Some innate trust might form despair acute
enough to swim the sea that has no other shore.

Intentions tired love-bright Cherry flowers
to falling petals, the moon-phased tide
inadvertently carried out to Sea,
and intellectual comprehension
remained a dismal opium agonist.

A stubborn egocentric disposition preserved
by camphor in a half-forgotten attic settled
beneath the dust of earthquakes of timely disillusions.

The changes in insight and perception
through sorrow or harmony remain
as proof of having survived despair
or bounced along upon elastic air.

All roads led only to destruction,
it is the way of roads.
There is no peace to be found outside of Nature,
there is no peace beyond the innate nature.

It may come as a grace the Sea or Forest grants,

a revelation after years of picking locks,
a disillusion when all ways end where they began
and meaning has with sleight of hand to be infused
in failed ascents or Stoic resignation
as it all is kiff-kiff in the end.

III

The Indo-European dream defying death —
imperishable fame by courage, song, cognition.
The joy of breathing in the Earth beneath the Sky,
the joy of doing what could not be done,
the joy of creating that which did not exist
and vie with Nature or the joy of striving
to give a token back in gratitude for life.

The moonlight quickening in night dark pupils,
the skipping fawn raising dawn-red waves in Rosebays,
mellifluously interwoven features
of thoughtscapes and cloudscapes,
the shades of green in leaves of springtime forests,
the features of mountain peaks black clouds keep changing,
the silence, the murmur, the roaring of the Sea,
the steadily evolving interaction
of various species with Nature and each other,
a metaphor however fine-grained could
only suggest as a coarse-grained fleeting shadow
in glitter-gray soaked sand in a lull between two waves.

Each slough shedding, at Dawn or Dusk,
a threadbare habit of verbal innovation,
intent on discovering the only given way
and hone the blunted edge of compass true precision,
etherealise the phonemes of suggestion,
though only to acknowledge with reluctant wonder,
humour or regret that every single rung
in purgatorio awareness left
the current phraseology as outgrown clothes
however newly cut to measure.

The quest for lip and tongue-wrought sounds to cast
a spell that would invoke the dread and wonder
of infinitely interlaced harmonies —
a pilgrimage compulsive, without hope or end.

Trying to fathom the full-blown extent
of days and nights that passed each other
as waves that surged in across the sand
and sank back grateful for having been conceived
by winds of ceaseless change
and reabsorbed in their common origin
amounted to an attempt
fostered by vanity, innocence or hybris
to skip along the snowy peaks of bliss
and be as Nature always is —
absolute for death.

IV

Meaning reveals itself in the ruffles
the pirries colour the mirror of the Sea,
in that embrace that keeps the breath at bay.

Between two thoughts,
between two breaths,
between two lips —
the yawning abyss
that calls as Seirēnes sing —
the Tiger *aouṃ* left silence.

V

While scuttling to and fro across the oak-beam deck
of Bellerophon the dying sunlight gilds
the cliffs of Bretagne, his victories of glory —
his visions that vanish past horizons lost in blue.

Feeling through the body all three-and-twenty wounds

as fear and hate of friends and foes, as *karmă*
the fifteenth of March, he regrets his scepsis,
the flight from nothingness that drove the ambition.

Huddling in the doorway to Notre Dame at midnight,
sheltered from the snowstorm, Wolves, the gallows tree,
through shivering heart horrors and bittersweet relief
he knows nought but this that death consumes all life.

Wishing this at death that its dawning light
would splinter all the limits of the Universe
he waits and waits an aeon of an instant
for the bliss of grace.

With humour and fury when ill with mortal fever
he bequeathes her the next best bed
in which she conceived and bore the twins,
in which they died, in which he would as well.

Now past the Gate of Tears, in the long hot night
he knows the pain is ceaseless, the growing fame illusive
compared to the genuine deals with diamonds,
with ivory, rifles — and with rattling chattel.

Each Chanticleer calling compulsively find
reasons for celebrating himself
in the cozy realm of his chosen roost,
innocent and unaware of all the Earth,
the multitude of stars and constellations
that would rob him of his cherished throne of meaning.

VI

September tinted sunrise, mists that thread
its dew-drop jewels on wheeling galaxies
of spider spins revealing webs of death
until the slanting light from the peevish sun
restores the universal exchange of energy
on which all life depends.

Winking above the leaf-dark skyline —
consciousness potential evolution.

The future once lay open in space as well as time —
an infinite bounty — to grant the Universe.

Reviewing now the roller-coaster days and nights,
the ocean trenches of magnetic despair,
the tingling touches of infinity,
the thrills of lightning blue epiphanies,
conceptions that attempted to camouflage or cure
with woollen vicuña shreds of words
the icy flails of sleet,
the pinpricks of frost that made the fingers numb,
the blinding beating of the midday Sun
upon the black anvil of oval desert stones —
chiselled in neurones for a human while,
and vanishingly present in a light cone,
sorrow, humour and regret prevail.

Silence remained
the option of integrity
as music failed.

The luscious trust in timely traditions,
the stony ground that stands
the courage to fight disasters,
the option to leave a life or death behind
for that which might hide behind the twin dimensions.

Another day in which to wait or soar
up into the cold wet tongues of drifting clouds
and follow the Autumn call to fly away.

The sonorous yearning,
the air a neutron star,
vocalic crunching timbre —
khraouuṅ khraouuṅ khraouuṅ.

Resounding spell response
polyphonic unison,

synchronised emotions.

Clear guttural rainy calls of keen affection
intensifying harmony in April,
tuning devotion into one another.

This dawn-fresh rose could not but bloom forever,
this blood-dark rose would always spread the scent
of flowering woods and water-fragrant love,
this given symbiosis would with nature
always stay tetra-valent carbon clear.

Concrescent feelings that such intimacy
shaped far too vast and real a realm
to be explored by human lips and eyes
bestowed immortality on each panting breath.

Caresses and glances
pregnant with eternity,
the cradle of confidence
would rock and rock forever,
steadfast as an orbit in empty space
grounded in the universal cosmic truths.

VII

The wistful sadness of the fleeting moment
incensed by light green floral odours,
hovering some honey-happy heartbeats
to drain a Honeysuckle dry,
presaged the migration
when the shadows would lengthen,
and foreboded the final emigration.

Vanishing in sombre evening clouds
there is no more that can be said or done
to stay the flow of the blood of time,
leaving this earthly Heaven and each other
each bone in the body sorrow-aching lengthwise.

The runes of flying away in the Sky
alone, not together, will be invisible.

Now never more to whirl around each other
as inter-dependent binary stars,
not even to be transformed by gravity
and fuse for a universe to one black whole still being —
not even that — but cease to be aware,
the memories of wounds and blessings
etched into each other
erased — the vacuum of interstellar space.

The last, the tentative death-wild kiss of life
withering the hearts with blue-black agony
to leave this light, to leave each other lost.

Embracing once more within as without
an instant swaying on the abyss' edge
before the backward extinction somersault
out into that which is not as it is.

VIII

The west wind howls along the shore and blows
the sand our feet shaped out across the Sea
and nothing will be seen and heard no more.

A fragment of an instant among aeons
allotted on the scene of Earth and Sea.

Feathers on the breath
of a storm from heaven
whisked away in one direction only
and kisses snatched in passing
from one eternity into another.

The Laurel crown on life that death vouchsafes,
the icy blessing of oblivion.

A lack of courage to stay newborn

bare and be mother-naked for the darkness.

Two mirrors facing each other could be raised
at birth and death by time
to amplify the fury and the sound that echoed
throughout this stage of fools, a human while,
and show the stasis of immortality.

But this ethereal sweetness
in rain drops on the lips,
could be a nudge in the side from an echo
coming from somewhere far away,
a gooseflesh shiver of prognostication.

The silence beyond the noise of living beings —
to live a life begets immortal longings.

IX

The written was already there,
the sharp and sudden pin prick
when reaching out to you among
the yellow straws in the haystack.

The Mountains

I

Semantic categorisation,
vivisecting the whole,
default mode network fragmentation —
the misery left when it fails to feel alive.

II

A wall of words alienates
the world from seeing and sensing.
The denotation and the connotations
conjure up a metaphoric atmosphere
infused and shaped by the prior impressions,
sorrow or love, disgust, fear, wrath, or wonder,
which best can crystallise the nascent facets
of colour, tone and timbre.

Words may alleviate loneliness —
blue Sky flying silky summers
borne away from the lips
on the wings of a morning wind
to an unknown other in the evening,
or rise as sighs in the wilderness
to ravines, Ash trees, and rivers
to listen, accept and forgive.

The phonemes of 'river'
are not the same as the purling flow
of oxygen and hydrogen atoms
that rush down towards the Sea
to be quickened by the Sun
for yet another cycle
or to drift above
the ribbed-long sand of the seabed in the dark
as a four-degree cold current.

The signifying sounds
and signs — which evoke

caresses, colours, and sounds
of boisterous springs and waterways,
clear soothing trickles under leafy Apple Trees,
thundering cataracts of torrents,
green-fresh water fragrance, airs
of river running sensed, heard, touched and swum —
may also fling the portals of a past lap-open,
revealing how once upon a time
it felt when becoming the water
of one particular river at one particular instant
alive as that river's very water,
at one with the *Naïades*
as ever-changing eddies,
as soft and solid flowing
being moving water.

III

Alone, a lynx-eared silence listens.
The sense of being here and now expands
to encompass all that which is.

Mutual silence may
transcend communication
to be communion when
becoming aware of one another
no longer lost in space and time.

IV

Sloe and Cherry snow
flowering fringe the forest,
Forget-me-not and Buttercups
lightening green grass meadows.
The bounty of the Earth,
an infinite variety
contrasting or harmonious —
the wonder of each single point and present.

Curlew trills ripple and web away
as imperceptible echoes,
ocean waves gnash shingles
against each other to grains of sand,
each single heartbeat of the Sea, each song
quantises the flow of time.
A fleeting span
allotted by evolution.

Faint stars fade at the winks of twilight,
heaven flowers a rose-scenting Dawn.

Sunset's wistful slant-light deepen into dusk,
dusk darkens, a vast and sky-black night,
the firmament spreads out the wings to fly
immortal yearning up towards the stars.

It must all cohere
in interdependent unison.

V

The burden of sustaining the sojourn
here, a human while,
enduring the dissonance of ceaseless thoughts,
the terror of activity forged goals,
the struggles with the bane to find a purpose
while trudging down a smooth-paved urban road
of preordained determination,
almost forgetful of the local blinkers.

Day-nights sand the senses as drouth of khamsin blasts
and shifts the sun-bleached frames
of shipwrecked loves a little further up shore.

Still struggling in the threadbare standard armour,
still strolling around the well-worn garden paths
of passion, hope or fear
that once were virgin wild,
blood-red, leaf-green or granite with despair,

weary of waxing and waning yearly seasons
that with the sun hand scorch all they can reach
and sprinkle balm with the moon hand's fingertips.

VI

By fusing the pearly Sky with the bluish haze
of the Sea in front of the forestay sail
the eery calling at dusk and dawn
that sometimes resounds behind the horizon
leaves sooner or later no alternative.

Once safely past the noise-soiled plains,
the many stuck in exile from themselves
ceaselessly striving to allay
the gnawing emptiness by activity,
deploring this hapless plight, but passing on
to the fine-tuned lightening of the strain
in mountain loneliness and altitude,
toward a tardy return to that which is
and was once the Sky being blue infinity,
the grass more green than green,
each pumice stone a world set adrift among the sedges.

Abruptly needling hairpin bends,
one half of the track rain-washed away,
each breath now deep and quick in the edge-thin air.

The smooth perpendicular cliff below,
the hollow nudge in the pit of the guts,
the urge to feel the uplift of the air
by shedding the safety harness of fear
and like the Lammergeier soar along
a cloud of snow beneath the poppy Blue.

Long thin bridges swinging
in black-green slime-moulded ropes
of grasshalms, crossing cracked ravines
with torrents of glacial waters —
a wrong step would prevent the next.

Each slow turn by each slow twist,
a pilgrim's tunnel vision
transcending the zenith
of looming icy peaks.

Guttural croaks come rolling through the ravine,
two Ravens circling overhead enwrapped
in shrouds of snowflakes which paint the gray sky white,
keep searching for a mortal dying or cold dead
but warm enough to be pierced with pointed beaks.
Cloud swirling drifts submerge the mountain ridges,
frore air has forced Black Bears to hibernate,
short light, honed frost sends Conifers to sleep,
Thar and Argali plough drifts of snow away
from yellowed grasses with keen cloven hooves.

These knee-deep footsteps without a trace at dusk,
still breathing heavily in the airless air,
the unknown deviation of the mountains,
frail trust in the pointing of the inner needle,
visions transform themselves with recollection.

The sentinel Cedars stay immovable
identically camouflaged with pillowy profiles,
waiting for the greening light and rain in April.
The atmosphere ether-thin, no trace of earthly smells,
but snow, snow warming the blood like eiderdown.

Forgetting each foul regret, each cherished glimpse,
bereft of the lifebelt *mantraḥ* of high hope —
tomorrow and tomorrow and tomorrow.

Snow absolves constraints of obligations,
conceals causality and three dimensions —
hearing now the crane-grey light singing in the air,
adrift and carefree in the ninth wave's snowdrift.

The dread felt blessing of snow,
the flame-white peace of oblivion
granting absolution from identity,
absorbed in the universal white of nothing.

On the way through the air from the clouds
continuously symmetry creating
snowflakes flow lighter than thoughts,
each one unique, a crystalline cathedral,
at larger scales, a realm
forged in another dimension
by the fey wand of the frost, but losing later
its structure by compression
till the flower Sun of Spring
dissolves its identity in a drop of water.

VII

There — duck and drake through the shifting veils
a dim grey shade approaching ineluctably —
a season turning day to night
or night to day,
and softly as each snowflake falling from the Sky,
a fellow mortal in these wilds of whiteness,
alone, not social in a pack, like Wolves —
comes meandering down from the glacial heights,
aware of gravity and buoyancy,
aware of being beyond this place and instant.

The full-plumed tail, the broad paws print the snow
until new snowflakes with finger-tipping brushes
only leave impressions of the past as memories.

Rainbows of tears and laughter in the valleys —
stark black and white in winter naked mountains.

A shape of snow
inhaling air, exhaling mist
as sprays of flowers
dissolving in the silence,
nestled in spins of moths and hairs of goats,
with trust in whatsoever fate
will grant to rush the blood sun red,
at rest, a human while beside
the shielded whiff-sprayed cliff.

Indistinct in the white light-whirling haze
a reifying shadow
is quickening to a vast and gray-bright presence.
The Spirit of the Snow High Mountains
sliding round crevices and rocks as pirries,
savouring the cold keen air with humid nostrils,
approaches through the ethereal froth
of fragile crystal leaves
conceived in the womb of winter frost clouds,
towards the marking cliff,
susceptibly cautious of a strange unknown,
drawn forward by each heartbeat's thrill to see
a furry faced snow drift alive with dew-green eyes.

At the mutual wilderness distance
the long thick fluffy tail
was curling up for warmth and cover.

The snowflakes patchily muting
the densely spotted guard hairs'
mottled unison of autumn leaves.

Fearless serenity — coming
as cold-spun whirls of snowflakes,
at one with the weather
and the granite bedrock
of live tectonic thrusts.

A quickly thickening down — snow-frozen air,
each snow-flake feathery moth-winged to be weightless,
melting on icicle lips to height-cold water,
transparently sweet on the tip of the tongue —
and the growing clarity —
a noiselessly roaring avalanche.

Apart from the turning of the stars,
the burden of thoughts, the bubble burst illusions,
the iron-railed direction of the will —
the distance stretching out
towards the anonymous rocks,
the powder-sprinkled ghosts of Cedars —

was a lightly disappearing spare dimension —
impalpable touches through palpable air,
a sudden sense of one another,
a recognition of that which is as it is —
the awe-sprung beauty,
the solemn grace of the snow-capped eyebrows,
the coat's ground colour consonance,
the naked nose — a pink moth twin pitch spotted.

The sonorous purring rising and ebbing,
ingressive and egressive phased to lull
the sea to a halcyon mirror of the soul,
a healing music from the sphere behind
the dimethyltryptamine pulsating scend.

Communion beyond the pulse of the blood,
the mutual origin, common consciousness.
White peace of snowflakes
as far as eyes and ears may ken —
the natural wonder
that is absolute.

The ice-blue turquoise iris-smiling eyes,
the pupils' luminous night infinity
glowing through the air's
ceaselessly shedding of snowflakes' lace-veils —
past time — eternity at the speed of light.

VIII

The stealthy warning from the winter mountains,
the graying light of the gibbous afternoon.

Full of an earthly fill
of the source that has no source,
stretching out the joints to wear out weariness,
shaking off the snow coats to rise in unison
and vanish as thinning mists
behind each single snowflake.
The way through the mountain passes to a lair,

the way to warmth and shelter in a timber shed,
two different ways towards the one and only fate
with visions of each other in an instant shorn of time.

Skipping on light air through the heavy snowdrifts,
brushing by a deeply bowing branch
the needles of a Cedar luminously green-blue.

The self-same snowy mountainscape
shimmering imperceptibly with inner light.

IX

Spring, Summer, Autumn, Winter,
the innate fine-tuned correspondence,
and each experience a new metamorphosis,
the quest for meaning that ceases to matter
following fate, the west wind, or cross currents —
diaphanous to the touch of light and darkness.

The joy, the sorrow, the pleasure, or the pain
of every present awareness of three seconds —
the end and beginning of a journey.

X

A naked voice cannot contrive,
it must follow the grain of the wood.

The yearning to create
at Dawn and Dusk —
the twilight hours of transformation —
sensible shapes of sounds.

Spontaneous recognition —
conscious imagination.

Writing in the wetted sand between two waves

or in the wave that washes out the written,
the self-same wish to feel at one with Nature
and give a token, at least, of gratitude.

Each bottle launched at sea
a bubble of vanity or hope.

Silence stays truth white,
art flaunts peacock feathers.

Endeavours that strive to reach the absolute
resignation will embalm within a pearl.

XI

The written was writing itself by tracing
the light blue lines already etched into the air.

The Pit

From borough to borough in the global city
the wretched strive to reap the profit of their treason
against themselves, the forest green, the blue-sky sea,

heedless of having been blessed from birth
with *dé* self-insight, gnōsis, *svabhāvaḥ,*
like Sticklebacks, Ash trees, Tigers, and Fin whales.

So never to see the light there of the day
would be the preferable option.
and ceasing to exist would be far better
than dreaming of a life that ought to have been lived,
but fear, conformity, or indifference
postpone the pointed dagger till tomorrow till tomorrow.

A stone-enclosed species, obsessed and possessed
by blinding illusions, ingenious gadgets,
constructs a common commercial madhouse.
Gnawed hollow by anxiety the inmates
run round in their confines of concrete and glass,
searching for something, not knowing what,
with both ears lead-lidded by scree-slides of traffic,
taking their blinkers for granted, not knowing
nought else, torn rootless by alienation,
the days rush by restless, the nights slug by sleepless.
Phosphorescent vampires ransack beds and crossroads
for wounded who still smell of human blood.
and cannibals impeccably disguised as undertakers
relieve consuming anguish of inwit emptiness
by gorging themselves on swollen corpses
the soil has tenderised with plastic-spiced poisons.

Steadily fleeing the present,
the terror of the icy breath of death,
licking the neck with a tendril soft forked tongue
awareness benumbs itself in entertainment,
in febrile activity of meaningless work
that has the power to confer oblivion
as long as being maintained compulsively.

Anonymous offices, factories of noise

and ceaseless eruption of things
from production volcanos deaden the land,
smoke from scorched earth scratches the eyes
of those who still can weep to wring out tears.
High vacuum coffins hover over ruins
of concrete and ashes for the final shivers
of inadvertent habits.

Societies hurtle down the slope to extinction,
unconsciously sensing vague ominous dangers
lurking behind the corner of each hour.
And advertisements wrap up stars in winding sheets
to hide the living infinity of space
that might have nudged a seed of hope to grow.

The poor can crisscross the streets on crutches
as fair game for assassins
on four screeching wheels of teeth-gnashing aggression.

Though rainwater ripples in winds of light
the angle features of a child
stiffen in time to a stoning grimace
displaying the ghost of wizened emotions —
wonder, care, and compassion.

Silence has turned into torture
as surreptitious obstruction
against the common good
of cacophony conformity.

The rainbow of the seasons shifts from gray to grey,
the melodies of night and day sound like each other,
evil and good are indifference synonyms
and death resembles life as life resembles death.

The fungi and bacteria
in soils that nourish plants
are burnt to wring out ore for rosaries and orders.

There is no silence in the air for music
or peace in minds for thoughts or emotions;

ceaseless explosions to exploit all resources
erode inspiration and blunt the senses.

The future is gangrened to pass the time
with vapid amusements as anodynes.
Automatic jaws chew to smithereens
the tasteless corpses from factories of slaughter.

Intricate complexity,
patterns far beyond equilibrium
may yet appear as unconscious shadows.

The unique characteristics of children
are plucked out by relentless vivisection
in daylight muting institutions
to turn them into gears to fit conveyor belts
and mimic conveyor belts in robotic actions.
Identity sacrificed for bland nonentity.

Cutting down the sacred groves of Black Poplars
the crowds build palace halls hallowed to consumption
and stuff themselves with all things that exist,
but end up eating sand, rocks, air, and filth
till nothing is left but to consume themselves.
Black days and blinding nights — the curse of the Earth.

Exiles, tame or psychotic,
stuck in layers of tightly stacked boxes
keep screaming in speckled despair,
beyond expression, to Pegasus or Cygnus,
who cannot hear or heed such agony —
a grain of dust in the vastness sphere of parsecs.

And money cannot smell, the *mantraḥ* of bankers
trying to wash the blood streams off their hands
while financing wars, enslavement, extortion.
for money stinks like a year-old Ostrich egg
exploding in the desert sun to cause
instantaneous continuous vomiting.

Soaring up towards the sky-blue infinite

a child's philosophical curiosity
is shot down by the monsters of convention
so, she or he can end life as a mummy
stuffed up by taxidermists who for hire
quite unawares thus take revenge
for their own childhood mutilation,
comfortably convinced they have no other choice.

And yet at midnight
the harvest Moon may haul
a broken heart home
with hempen ropes of gravity.

Miserable prisoners and outcasts,
crumb sacrifices offered
to let the *bien-pensant* majority
feel better off, just so that they can wallow
in superfluous mire of abundance
and thus, distinguish themselves
from the lost and the naked
who shiver with hunger in the wetted wind.

The new day, which also dawns in factories
and offices, descend from the sky, a spirit
of smiles and boundless promise, but is slowly
anaesthetised to wither away by inattention.

Each hour becomes a close-read yellowed leaf
before it can unfold to green in sun and rain.

Discrediting the warnings of the weather
the crew of the Arc Titanic fights fiercely each other
to don the most extravagant and flashy uniforms.
the passengers are fast asleep or drowsy
if not absorbed in busyness
or playing poker, mesmerised by gain and loss.
A few frenetic fools dart round the deck and point
in wild despair to the mountain of an iceberg
that looming in over the starboard prow extends
down nine times deeper below the glassy surface.

The eyes and lips of individuality
are sealed by common jealousy or hatred—
the concrete that makes members of groups stick together.

Coarse egocentric stags prance to and fro.
The males of the species bristling competition,
admiring themselves in the chrome-glass of their toys,
jealous of others with more blinding illusions,
contemptuous of those whose toys are old or broken,
reeling with self-conceit, ale, and resentment
against all females who make them superfluous,
grow obsolete and stale like worn-out news,
not ripe with self-awareness.

But sometimes at evening
in an outlawed lull of silence
a choir of children purifies the air
awhile in a moss-grown dilapidated church.

No here, no now, just trite considerations
lacking the fragrant scent of Spanish Jasmines
that dew-drenched dawn before the Moon had set.
the spray of the waves in the thirty-six-knot wind
pierced by the screams of a flock of Black-backed Gulls
who pecked at the wounds of a washed-up Gray Seal pup.

Integrity — a bearing buried with religion.
Clinging to their preconceived ideas
as if to lifebelts
coteries of logical positivists
explain the worlds away that transcend their intellects —
for there is naught here but this scrappy corner
nook in our windy attic where we creep
together awaiting annihilation,
a few missing pieces which science will unravel
as grounded in physics, the rock-solid level —
that grows more insubstantial and abstract
the deeper the delving, atoms, quarks, and bosons,
entangled particles' synchronicity,
the all-potential emptiness
that tunes the four fundamental forces

to balance in absolute harmony,
one chance in seventeen billion billions,
or just the *léger de main* of a hidden Joker.

Solemn and sombre Academics
trip down through marble halls of polished pillars,
more timid than church mice, consumed by research
to prove themselves the epitomes of *Grübelsucht*;
searching for the unique universal system,
dissolved in the ether of abstractions,
distilling meaning out of absurdities,
they do not live their philosophies but stage careers,
hedging their bets with camouflaged loopholes,
paid panders to parasitic
syndicates of limitless profit,
hell-bent on vanity and worldly fame,
but praying for the miracle that such anomalies
somehow will prove to be shortcuts to meaning.
If ending up swaddled down in sparkling purple,
consecrated by obsequious esteem,
they gulp down their wages of ash-gray acrid dust
or munch them with mealy mouths and bone-dry lips,
though tempted half-consciously to regret at dawn.

The majority construct new murder weapons,
sarin, plutonium, supersonic missiles.
Forgive them, but there will be no one left
to grant them forgiveness in the future
apart from some crumbling skeletal remains
nourishing lichens and bacteria.

The nondescript computer technician
protected in plastic sheets and stainless steel,
feels free like a weathervane in prevailing winds,
and sees no alternative, not knowing any better,
not knowing what to do, because he has
a neutral *tabula rasa* mind
chemically purified of conscience
the better to attract
the Blow Flies of the senseless algorithms.
The microfausts of applied technology

fail to configure by whom they have been bought.

The soft red light of Dawn
sustains a willow sapling
in a vacant lot, and each green leaf,
a beauty sublime, a joy too keen to be
beheld for any length of time —
contrasting nature with the human lot.

The species pay, for reshaping the world
in its image, with sanity, soul, and self.

The common chameleonic prostitute,
the political agent — cocooned in a cage
of gold and granite, security, and guards,
covertly busy within his cosy compass
of wheeling and dealing, allegiance change,
betrayal and bribery — remain dead certain
that sooner or later he can make a deal
with Earth to suspend the laws of Nature
a little here or there for the benefit
of his party to corner the coming election
and carry on as always with rules time regulations
that steal from the future to surfeit the present.

Aesthetics and ethics, the leaf of life,
one side silver-downed, the other brilliant green.

The prototypic human tries to discover
the meaning of life by worshipping machines
as omniscient oracles, designed
to tease responsibility out of shaking hands
and guarantee the comfort of uniformity
by making the devotees identical as zeros.
Gleichschaltung perfected, marching uniforms.
Algorithms that only can chew cud
on that which already has been digested
reduce the social media addict
to yet another copy of the copies.

God stays above the clouds and all is well
with the stars that follow their destinies in heaven,
the schizophrenics patent their brave new world on Earth.

Olives greening now on age-gnarled trees,
clusters of grapes turning purple in the sun,
wheat nodding ripe with golden ears,
the timbre resounding in a mother's voice
when calling her children home at sunset,
the care that fuses generations,
the sky-blue glancing of an elfin smile,
the chilling touch of a pair of blood-flushed lips,
the magic carpet of music absolute,
the note of seaweed wafting through gray, early air,
the dancing *Orestiades* clad in blue mountain mist,
the taste of black-shining clouds in oval raindrops
that fall upon the tip of the tongue,
the green ethereal scent of Tea-rose petals,
the close communion of love past time and space,
suggest the hidden all-pervading scend
of infinity-eternity
that charges every single routine habit
of turning days and spinning nights
with meaning enough to face the boar-tusked mask
that looms in the horizon of the future as an omen.

Reality evolves beyond the shallow confines
of algorithms, semantics and words, words, words,
beyond the public square of one and zero,
beyond the attempts of the left-brain hemisphere,
the anterior-posterior cingulate cortices
to force all the processes of the universe
into a static frozen puzzle
that could suggest a semblance of coherence,
though purged of human breath.

A system — frail intellectual crutches.
Integrity and wonder are kept alive by stumbling,
by scratches, blood and changing perspectives.

Surreptitious glints of empathy and care

from a partly hidden beacon peep all suddenly
through a crack in the grainy miasma —
a buccaneer dares abrupt and flashing glances
through a lattice of five fingers from the underworld of life.

Any decent member
among the congregation of the creed
of usury and profit, of getting more than giving,
pray with glowing keyboard to the temple
where moneys are created, hocus pocus,
straight out of the thinnest air of nothingness
by writing the ciphers of a number in machines
which buy and sell the debt of market slaves.

The self-destructive dystopia of automatic exploitation
where claws count chipped coins and bloodless lips mimic
the melody of winds in leaves and waves
by lisping numbers must not be anybody's business
and does thus, by definition, not exist.

The common groups of mere consumers,
ordinary inoffensive citizens
with sweet-toothed dreams and shark-toothed nightmares,
who waste their daylight on Earth by buying things
to disregard the steadfast inner tension,
too occupied or indifferent to care
about all issues that cannot be grasped
without prolonged attention, only want to leave
responsibility to whom it may concern,
and be relieved of knowing their fate in the future.

The ancient sacred rhythm of singing,
long and short syllables with pitch and timber,
united individuals in mutual response.

A fisher caught a holy Flounder who would promise
to grant each wish if left alive to swim the seas,
and so, he slipped him back in the ocean depth of darkness.
The wife of the fisher had worldly ambitions
and cursing her husband she went down to the Sea
to demand her due as his wedded wife.

"Just a pretty cottage beside this trickling ditch.
Just a decent house in a flower-happy garden.
Just an eagle castle perched on a mountain top.
Just a kingdom jewel set in the silver sea.
Just this whole sphere spinning round in space."

A sluggish fluid seeps slowly through the veins
and nameless fear anoints the piston strokes,
to be a machine the one and final goal,
to function as a faultlessly well-built steel machine,
to overpass Nature and become immortal
just like the gods of yore, *Titanes* and *Jötnar.*

Eternal life, but growing frail, decrepit,
not heeding the plight of *Tithōnos,*
the face, at best, a winter-wrinkled apple,
talking incessantly but saying nothing
as there is nothing left to say,
instinctively sensing the bliss of extinction,
but doomed just to renew the worn-out parts.

The wish to be omnipotent like God,
(no one is free but Zeus alone)
is thwarted desire for individuation,
akin to belief in being Christ or Caesar.

The lure of power —
a dopamine neurotransmitter reaction,
the fundamental evil,
the depth of the abyss, the ultimate disease
of a ghost which is haunted by a soul —
produces a more debilitating
addiction than all illegal
and legal drugs combined,
as power corrupts itself
and wrecks the world
in its wake as collateral damage.

To grasp it, to keep it,
there is nothing the maddened is not prepared to do,
famine, slavery, war, and ruin.

The bloodshed in history,
now dry as the paper left as a witness.

No one is not entitled to make the same mistake.

Judgements are *ad hoc* or subjective projections
without the empathy that is the saving grace
of life and the implicate source that has no source.

And if a notion of the numinous,
clearer than light, more real than pain or joy,
appear with the face of time and space
belief will steal the truth of experience
and incubate a genuine fanatic
bereft of self-irony and graceful humour.

The heathen or the giaour must be killed
to eliminate the external threat of doubt
that nurses the dormant inner seed.
And yet the blue, green, grey, or purple Sea
containing all minerals and salts,
is present in every cell in the body
like the pulse of the waves
that is present in each breath.

The total annihilation engineered
by profit unlimited, universal greed —
a *Fenris* wolf that only can be satisfied
by eating up itself as nothing else is left.

The wages of defying the truth of Wine
are limbs torn apart, mutilation and death.

Either lack of meaning or peace in harmony,
music, emotion, the boundless realm,
or lies and religion, oil upon the seas.

The lowest common denominator,
the democratic ideal of dumbing down.
Democracy presupposes self-awareness
and limitless responsibility —

the pervasive influence of each excited field,
the intricate reciprocal evolution.

The being that did not want to see the light
just chose to turn back home — alike migration.

The Fox that sometimes came to sniff
around the barn in winter fog and twilight
but left his footprints as tokens in the snow
has found his fate in the road of accidents.

The ambient temperature of society:
greed multiplied by fear, this sum divided
by apathy multiplied by ignorance.

There is but one way out of the labyrinth
and meaning is never to be found outside the self,
and selves are rain drops from clouds
condensed from the vapor of the Sea.

This is a war disguised in camouflage
of solemn words, shrill screams,
and frozen apathy, willful ignorance,
a war more fateful
than all the wars of the past time each other,
the final war of *Homo semi-sapiens.*

And yet a sense of something strange and chilly
seems still from time to time at dusk or dawn
in secret to be smuggled through the bourne
at Planck-scale levels as anomalies
perfecting the laws of Nature.

Any species or individual
who chooses to neglect a yawning abyss,
a proven truth, a forest fire, chooses death.
The whisper of the onshore wind in the sedges.
The thunder of the surf of the Sea on the reefs.
The lights of the stars in their choir round Polaris.

Love - the blessing of a newborn child,

a gift from life, a sky-blown flower,
so fair and natural as the rising Sun.

The wear and tear on Earth and Sea
of more than eight thousand million
of one single species of insatiable mammals —
a self-destructive triumph
over the limits and laws of evolution.

Bacteria, fungi, insects, plants can only
thrive in mutual interdependence.
If one is forced into extinction
the other three will likewise die,
and so will all terrestrial life
who must depend
upon them for survival.

Basic ecological communities
collapse from east to west, from north to south,
increasingly with accumulating effect,
now cities are not left alone in burning up,
the tectonic plates of Earth are holocausts.

Ashes to ashes and dust to dust,
the democratic will of the general.

This epitaph may now not even be
chiselled in fair winds and running water,
so only a few and paltry fragments,
trivial, self-evident, and plain,
disfigures the processed remains of once green trees.

Nothing does here cohere,
menscliches, allzumenschliches.
Neti — *na iti* — not thus — not thus at all.
E quindi uscimmo a riveder le stelle.

There is just this,
the one and only single story,
the distant horizon that moves
in front of the lonely pilgrim on his Way

toward the same assumed potential
as in Dandelions, Elephants and Curlews.

Niels Hammer

Born in Denmark, Niels Hammer has lived in
various countries in Europe, the Middle and
the Far East, sailed the seas, established a
biological diversity refuge, and written in
journals, literary magazines etc.

Journals:
Mind and Matter
Journal of the Royal Asiatic Society
Zeitschrift der Deutschen Morgenländischen
Gesellschaft, about consciousness research
Indo-European linguistics and comparative aesthetics

Magazines:
Orbis, Littoral Magazine
Dream Catcher

Monograph:
The Art of Sanskrit Poetry, about Indian
poetics/aesthetics, the power of suggestion
and the ineffable.

9 781774 033852